THE GREAT CHEESE ROBBERY

CHRIS MOULD

ALADDIN
New York London Toronto Sydney New Delhi

ALADDIN
An imprint of Simon & Schuster Children's Publishing Division
1230 Avenue of the Americas, New York, New York 10020
First Aladdin paperback edition June 2018

Originally published in Great Britain in 2015 by Hodder Children's Books
Published under license from the British publisher
Hodder & Stoughton Limited on behalf of its publishing imprint
Hodder Children's Books, a division of Hachette Children's group
Also available in an Aladdin hardcover edition.

Cover designed by Karin Paprocki
Interior designed by Mike Rosamilia
The illustrations for this book were rendered in pen and ink.
The text of this book was set in New Century Schoolbook.
Manufactured in the United States of America 0519 OFF
2 4 6 8 10 9 7 5 3
Library of Congress Control Number 2017957347
ISBN 978-1-4814-9115-0 (hc)
ISBN 978-1-4814-9114-3 (pbk)
ISBN 978-1-4814-9116-7 (eBook)

For
Captain William Fred Tippey

BUTTON
LILY
THE BASEBOARD MICE

CAPTAIN
CRABSTICKS

OLD UNCLE NOGGIN

JONES

MR. DREGBY

CONTENTS

The Old Junk Shop

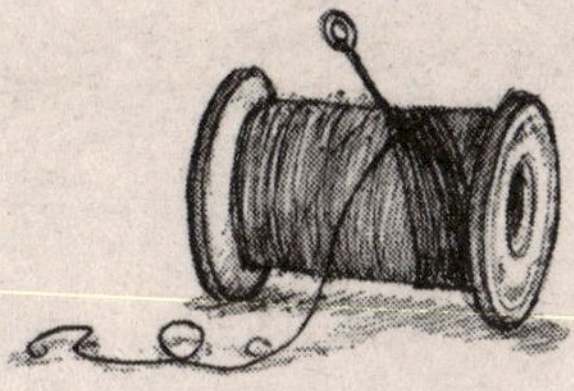

At the end of the street is an old junk shop. It's gloomy and shabby and nothing ever happens there. At least, that's what most people think. . . .

Among the odds and ends and things of no use, a dusty ship in a bottle sits gathering cobwebs on a shelf. But when the world isn't watching, a tiny pirate crew comes out to explore.

And when you're smaller than a teacup, a junk shop can be a pretty dangerous place. . . .

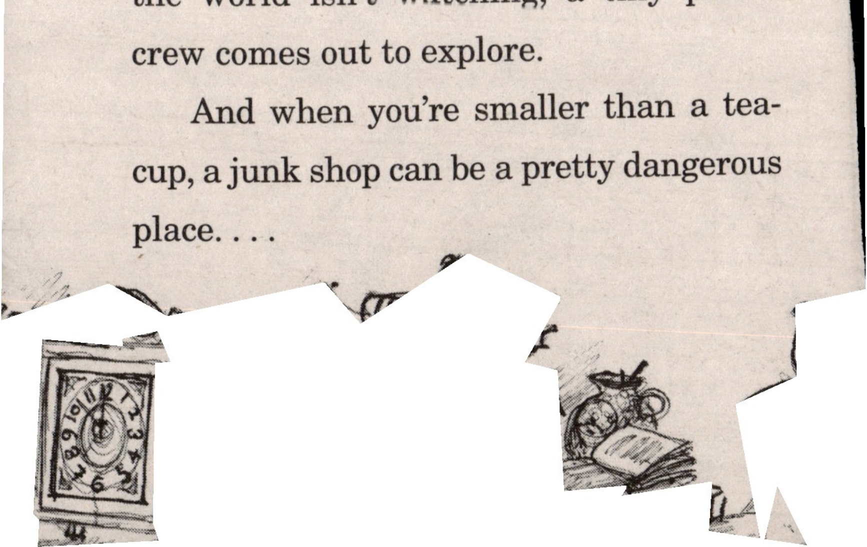

Shelf Life

Button the ship's boy had spent most of the afternoon exploring. He'd climbed in and out of piles of books and boxes of this and that to see what he might find. He'd even snatched a quick nap inside the old cuckoo clock.

But on his way back down to the shelf, Button had caught the back of his jacket on an old picture hook and now he was hanging helplessly on the wall.

"Oh, crumbs, not again," he said out loud to himself.

He looked over the shop. It was one of those perfect evenings. The moonlight was pouring in through the window and shone a silvery blue over the ship in the bottle. Everything had been calm until now. He tried to shake himself free, but it was no good.

High above Button, something had awakened in the dark. Mr. Dregby, the house spider, was eager to make a snack out of Button. He'd had his six eyes on the boy for some time. And now he could see that his perfect meal was hanging there beneath him, waiting.

"The young ones are the juiciest," Mr. Dregby cackled in delight.

Button heard a scritching sound above and he looked up in alarm. A tangle of long hairy legs and beady eyes was rushing toward him.

And then, all at once, he felt himself being pulled by the legs. He slipped clean out of his jacket and landed in a heap on

the floor, on top of his rescuer. She let out a muffled "YELP."

It was his best friend, Lily, the youngest of the pirate crew. She jumped to her feet, waving a long darning needle in Mr. Dregby's direction. The spider scuttled grumpily back into the darkness above the shelf.

"Thanks!" said Button as he straightened himself out. "That was close."

He looked up to see his coat was still hanging on the hook.

"You're not supposed to go wandering off on your own," Lily said. "It's dangerous!'

"I was looking for an adventure," Button replied.

“You shouldn’t wish too hard for an adventure,” said Lily. “You just might get one. . . .”

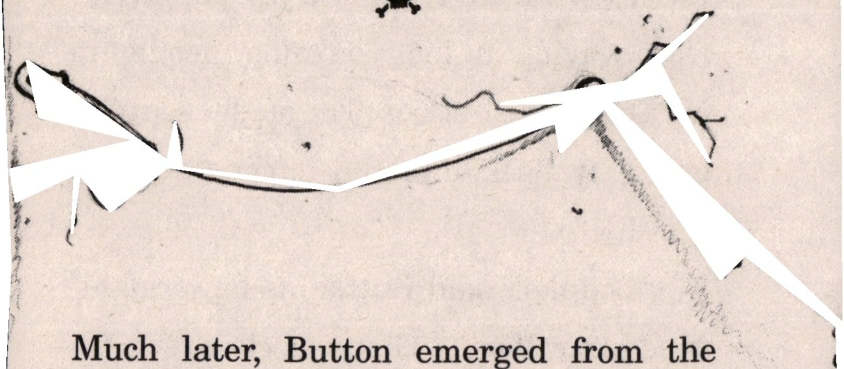

Much later, Button emerged from the ship, feeling calmer. He climbed out of the bottle’s glass neck and dropped down on to the shelf.

He took a good look around the shop. All was quiet again. From his pocket, Button pulled out a pirate flag, which he unfolded and tied between a candlestick and a pin in the wall.

"Captain's orders," Button explained to a nearby beetle. "It's my job to fly the skull and crossbones, and keep this shelf polished and scrubbed as properly as the deck of the ship."

Pepper Jack, the leader of the mangy gang of mice who lived behind the junk shop baseboard, was watching Button

from a distance, his mouse ears pricked. He nodded to Blue Vinny and Fleabag, two of his gang, as they waited in the darkness. Their mean eyes shone back at him through the black.

But Button couldn't see the mice. Instead he took a seat on a small cotton reel and kicked off his buckled shoes. Jones, the ship's cat, was curled up nearby, in a peaceful snooze. Lily was warming her hands at

the stub of a lighted candle and quietly singing a sea shanty to herself.

The captain of the ship, Captain

Crabsticks, was having a rest on an open page of his favorite book, *Treasure Island.* He was tired after a day on the hallway shelf reading *Domestic Pest Control* and *The Pocket Encyclopedia of Trees*, which wasn't pocket-sized at all. Especially not when you are two inches high.

"Arrr, there you are, me hearties," said Old Uncle Noggin as he hobbled along to join his shipmates. He took a sip from a steaming bottle cap of hot chocolate and pulled his blanket over his knees. He was sitting

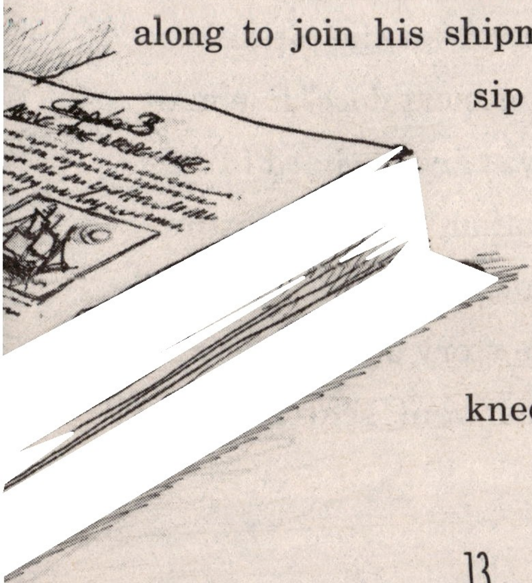

on his favorite seat, a dish sponge. "Are you ready for a good old pirate story?"

"Of course we are!" cheered Lily. She and Button loved Old Uncle Noggin's pirate tales, even though they weren't quite sure they were true.

"Is it made up?" Button asked. He was still undecided about the story of the cockroach who ate Captain Crabsticks's parrot, and the one about the pirate who sailed to the land of "next door" in a margarine tub . . . It was always hard to tell.

"Never you mind, young Button," muttered Old Uncle Noggin. "Tonight I'm telling you the story of Blackbeard's ghost, and how he went searching for

his missing head and found it bobbing around in the water like an empty barrel, glowing in the dark."

All eyes and ears were fixed on Uncle Noggin. The crew were so taken with the terrifying story of Blackbeard and his ghost, they weren't aware of a very real terror that lurked nearby.

They didn't hear sharp claws scratching their way up to the shelf, or the *whoosh* of tails whipping through the air.

They didn't see the sharp teeth and long twitching snouts that cast spiky shadows across the candlelit walls.

And that was *exactly* what the baseboard mice wanted!

The Base-board Mice

Button had once said to Lily that he didn't think the baseboard mice could talk. "Perhaps they always know what the others are thinking?" he'd suggested.

Luckily, he'd never got close enough to find out if he was right.

Now the mice sat silently in the darkest

corner of the shelf and waited as Uncle Noggin's tale came to an end.

"So he picked up his head, squeezed it firmly back into place, and wandered off into the darkness," finished Old Uncle Noggin. Then he took a gulp of his hot chocolate and watched the steam rise into the air.

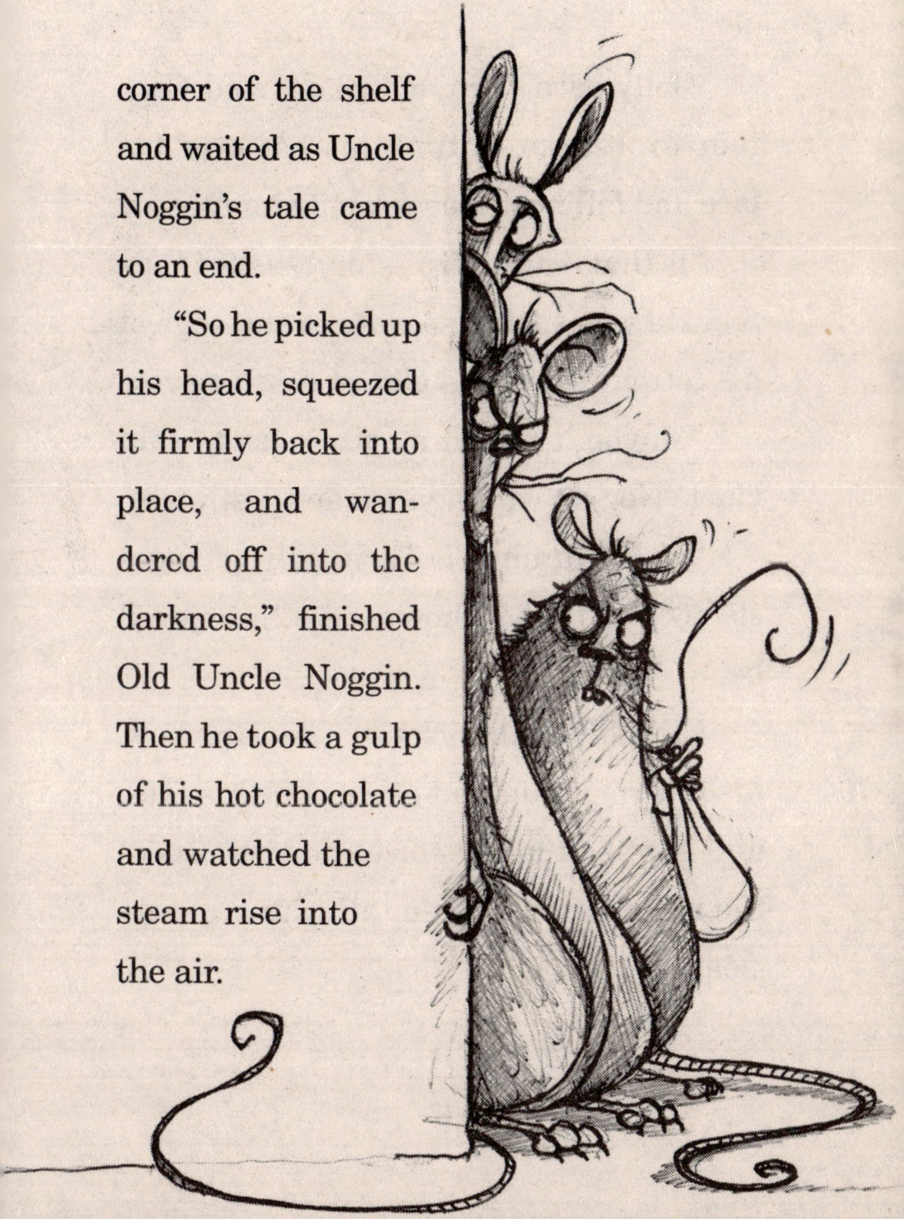

"Jolly good yarn, old chap," said Captain Crabsticks, putting his hat over his face and falling asleep in an instant.

"Is that *really* a true story?" asked Button. He was sitting so close to the edge of his cotton reel it was almost tipping over.

"Maybe it is and maybe it isn't," said Uncle Noggin with a yawn and a stretch.

"Well I think it *is*," said Lily, giving a sleepy grin to show how much she enjoyed being scared.

Captain Crabsticks was snoring now, his hat rising up and down over his face, and it wasn't long before the stillness of the night nudged them all into a gentle sleep.

Mr. Dregby the spider dangled by a thread above the snoozing pirates. He dropped slightly lower to get a clearer view and watched as the pointed shadows of the skirting-board mice came closer. Blue Vinny's long-fingered paws were carrying a bag made from a piece of old sackcloth.

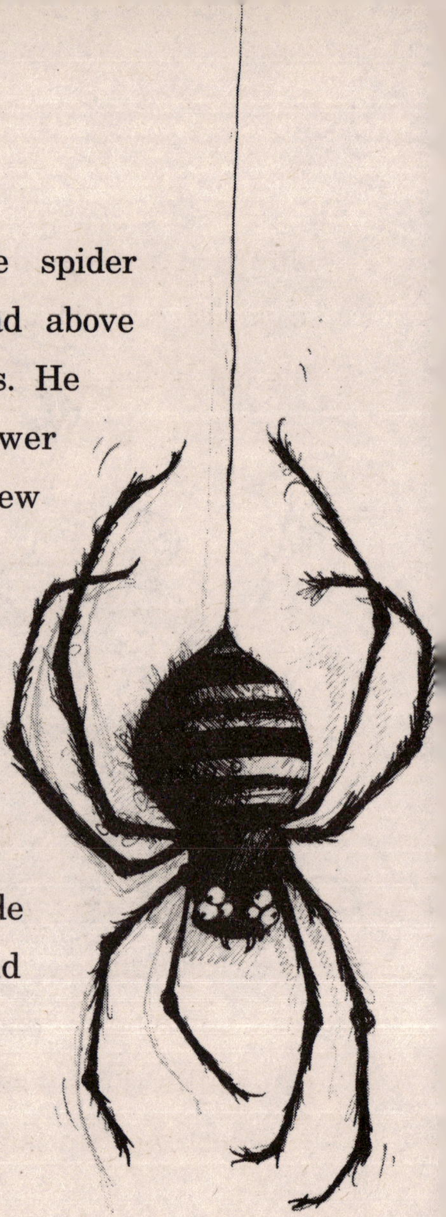

The mice swept down on Jones the

ship's cat and bundled him up tight in the sackcloth bag. Then off they went, across the old books, down the side of the long-case clock, and through the hole in the baseboard into their den.

"Those sneaky mice," the spider mumbled to himself. "They have no shame." He twisted himself around gracefully and whispered back up his thread into darkness.

It was some time before Button woke up. The candlelight was fading but he could see that where Jones had been sleeping peacefully, there was now an empty space.

Nothing unusual in that, Button

thought to himself. Jones was a cat, after all. He wandered far, and often. But as Button's eyes cleared of sleep, he suddenly noticed that in Jones's place lay a large blank envelope, waiting to be opened. . . .

Button called out for the others, then he picked up the envelope and peeled open the flap. Inside was a scratchy, scribbled drawing.

"What is it, Button?" said Lily, as the pirates gathered round.

"Cheese," said Button, "and I don't like it.'

"Nonsense," muttered the Captain. "Of course you do, all pirates love cheese."

“No, I mean I don’t like *this* cheese,” said Button.

“It’s a ransom note,” said Lily.

“Exactly,” announced Button. “A demand for cheese, in return for our poor, helpless ship’s cat!’

“Oh, I see . . . ” said the Captain, his

mind catching up slowly as they all stared in horror at the empty space where Jones had fallen asleep.

"And you know what that means, don't you . . . ?" Button continued. "If we want cheese, we have to go to the freezing cold place where it's always winter. The place they call . . . Fridge."

"But that's even further than the food cupboard," said Lily. "The journey is terribly dangerous. And even if we get there we'll never survive the frozen land of Fridge, let alone bring back a massive hunk of cheese. We've no chance."

"But we have no *choice*," insisted Button, staring at her through the fading candlelight. “We have to get Jones back, before they decide to eat him instead!”

“Well, you did say you were looking for an adventure,” Lily said, and she smiled a mischievous pirate’s smile. “This is a job for heroes. A job for the Pocket Pirates!”

There was a shout and a clatter and a terrible fuss below deck. Button's cries echoed around the glass bottle. Lily headed into the ship to investigate.

A pair of skinny pirate legs were sticking out of the old sea chest.

“Get me out!” cried Button.

“What are you doing?” asked Lily, dragging him by his ankles.

“Looking for this,” he said, and showed her the rolled-up paper he was hugging tightly.

"Umm, what is it?" Lily asked.

"Take a look," said Button excitedly. "It's the old map of the shop that Uncle Noggin found in a cupboard."

The young pirates decided it would be easier to read if they flattened it out, so they headed to the neck of the bottle. But flattening it was harder than they thought. The map kept springing back together and Button eventually disappeared inside it. It took Lily *and* Uncle Noggin to rescue him that time.

Captain Crabsticks appeared. He was pushing an old box filled with thumbtacks along the shelf.

"Crabsticks to the rescue!" he said.

“These should hold the pesky thing in place.”

Corner by corner, they held the map flat and pinned it in place. Lily kept the

thumbtacks still and Button jumped up and down to bang them in. "Take that!" he said, landing with a *thud*. "And that!"

"What ho," said the Captain. "Let's have a peep."

They all stood back and studied the drawing.

"We can head down the hallway into the kitchen," said the Captain, pointing his sword at the drawing of rooms and corridors. "We don't need the map. It's easy."

"No. We can't go that way," Button insisted. "Doyle's basket is just outside the kitchen. We'd be that gigantic mutt's breakfast before you could say blistering barnacles."

There was a sudden knocking sound.

"What's that?" asked Lily.

"Sorry," said Uncle Noggin. "It's me." He was shaking at the knees.

"I just remembered the day I fell in

Doyle's water bowl," he went on. "It was awful. . . ."

Button was only half listening. If they stopped to hear another of Uncle Noggin's stories, they'd still be here at midnight.

"What about this way?" said Button loudly, pointing to the corner of the shop where he knew a broken plug socket was hanging out of the wall. It meant they could squeeze into the gap between the wall, and if they could get through to the other side, they would be in the kitchen. He and Lily had been to the kitchen before. But they had never been to that cold and wintery place called Fridge.

"Maybe you could stay here and look after the ship," suggested Button, turning to Uncle Noggin.

"No chance," said Uncle Noggin, "I'm coming too. You can't do it without me. I'm Champion Cheese Lifter."

"Perfect," said the Captain. "In that case, you shall join us."

"Um, you're coming too, Captain?" Lily asked hesitantly.

"Of course, my dear girl," he bellowed. "A good pirate captain never abandons his crew!"

Button looked at Lily. She said nothing. Both of them knew that Captain Crabsticks and Uncle Noggin would slow

them down. But there was no stopping a pirate when they sniffed adventure.

"We shall head out first thing in the morning," said the Captain.

They had to get Jones back, and quickly.

A Perilous Journey

It's unlikely you would have looked through the junk shop window at six o'clock that morning. But if you had, you might have seen a crew of tiny pirates on the edge of a shelf, getting themselves ready for adventure.

They were armed with every weapon they could lay their hands on—safety

pins, sewing needles, cocktail sticks, and a jumble of other odds and ends inside their bags. Button had raised the flag as high as it would go.

"No one messes with this scurvy crew!" he cried. "We may be tiny, but we're still fearsome. Pocket Pirates to the rescue!"

In the corner of the shelf lay a tiny musical box with a wind-up handle. A long length of cotton was wound around the musical barrel so that when the handle turned and the music played, the cotton lowered to the ground. The pirates called it "the elevator."

They took it in turns. Captain first, of course. Then Uncle Noggin, then Lily.

And when the others were at the bottom, Button took one last look along the shelf, wound the handle once more and held tightly on to the end of the thread. He listened to the music play as he was lowered down to the next level.

From here it was a climb. Books were stacked in wonky piles, like giant, uneven steps. And though it was dusty and they had to help Uncle Noggin over all the thick encyclopedias and heavy car manuals, they soon reached the crockery box.

They tried to be quiet but the plates clattered noisily.

"Shhhhhhh," whispered Button. "You'll wake Doyle."

"Too late," Lily said with a gasp.

The sly eyes of the dog had blinked open. They could hear him heave himself out of his basket and head in their direction. Brushing his tail against the boxes and shelves. Sniffing the air.

"Crew! Hold still!" the Captain ordered. "That thing will have us for breakfast."

Doyle was moving closer.

"At least it means the mice will stay out of the way," said Lily.

"True," said Button. "But I don't like your chances against those teeth. . . . "

He looked over to the broken plug socket. It was only inches away. If they moved quickly enough they could squeeze

through into the gap in the middle of the wall, to safety. . . .

Button whispered his plan to the others. Captain Crabsticks and Uncle Noggin would go first, then Lily, and Button himself would bring up the rear. If they all went together, Doyle would be more likely to notice them.

"Marvelous plan, young Button," the Captain said, clapping him on the back. "Tally-ho!"

And off he went with Noggin in tow, the old pirate waddling as fast as his little legs would take him.

But even with Captain Crabsticks's help, Uncle Noggin was still painfully slow. Button gritted his teeth. The Captain had gone through the hole in the wall first, so that he could help Uncle Noggin from inside. But Uncle Noggin's plump belly was caught fast on the opening. The plaster crumbled around him.

Then, suddenly, Uncle Noggin was through. He took a chunk of plaster with him and made the hole bigger.

Lily darted after them and leaped gracefully into the hole. She turned and held her hands out to Button. But it was too late—Doyle had spotted him. Mornings were a bad time to come across the hairy beast. He was always hungry when he woke.

Button knew there was no time to think—he had to run for it, NOW! He could feel the dog's hot breath at his back as he sprinted toward the hole and threw himself through.

He looked over his shoulder, and saw a large black nose nudging at the opening. He'd just made it!

After all the excitement, the pirates

needed a rest. A slice of early morning light poured into the gap in the wall and they could just about see to unpack their pocket-size picnic. They perched on chunks of plaster, using their bags as

cushions. Uncle Noggin took off his neck scarf and laid it out to make a picnic blanket.

"Once, I got stuck in a teapot," began

Old Uncle Noggin as he handed out their breakfast of biscuit crumbs. "Wedged right in the spout, I was. I was thinner then, mind you. Wouldn't even get half-way down nowadays. Not with this." He patted his round belly.

"How did you get stuck in the first

place?" said Button, who had found a comfortable spot and was ready for a story as he ate his breakfast.

"Well, it started like this . . ." said Uncle Noggin. "I was out one night, heading toward a corner of a sandwich I'd spotted through the spyglass earlier in the day. I couldn't quite see from the ship but I was fairly sure there was a piece of chicken in there. Maybe even a dollop of mayonnaise if I was lucky. Anyway, off I went, into the night, when . . ."

Suddenly, a scratchy noise came from the darkness. It grew louder and louder. It sounded like legs marching toward them. Not just one pair of legs. Lots and lots of

legs. More legs than you can even imagine.

"What's that?" cried Lily and Button at the same time. Their hearts were beating fast and their eyes were open wide.

"Oh no," groaned Uncle Noggin. "Not again!"

"Woodlice!" Captain Crabsticks roared. "Abandon breakfast!"

But before anybody could move, the woodlice were upon them, scrabbling and fiddling and scratching. Around their feet, up on to their knees, snatching the biscuit

crumbs. Hundreds of them. Thousands of little feelers tickled the pirates' arms and legs.

Lily gave a muffled yell. "Gerroff my breakfast!"

"RUN FOR IT!" shouted Uncle Noggin and they all headed into the darkness.

A Place Called Fridge

The Pocket Pirates kept moving until the click-click-clicking of woodlouse legs had stopped. They could see a chink of light up ahead.

Button approached first. He climbed through the hole and found himself looking out into the kitchen. And right there

in front of him was the huge white door that led to the place called Fridge. Button looked up at the clock in the kitchen. It was nearly lunchtime. There's one way to get through a fridge door when you're two inches high, and that's to wait until a monster-size shopkeeper opens it. But the pirates couldn't hang around forever—they needed to rescue Jones as quickly as they possibly could.

"Perhaps a story will help pass the time," said Old Uncle Noggin, poking his head through the hole behind Button. "Did I ever tell you about the time when I was almost cooked alive in the microwave oven? It was a Monday morning and we hadn't eaten for three whole days. . . ."

"Errr, perhaps not now," said Button, wishing Uncle Noggin would concentrate.

Just then the dog bounded into the kitchen. He came racing toward them.

"We've been seen!" Button squeaked, and scrambled back through the gap in the wall.

"No, we haven't," said Lily calmly. "Look."

They stuck their heads out of the gap again and watched as Doyle skidded to a halt at the big white door. He rubbed his face against Fridge and barked excitedly,

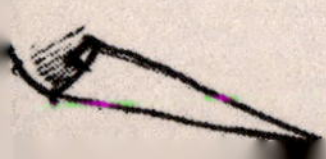

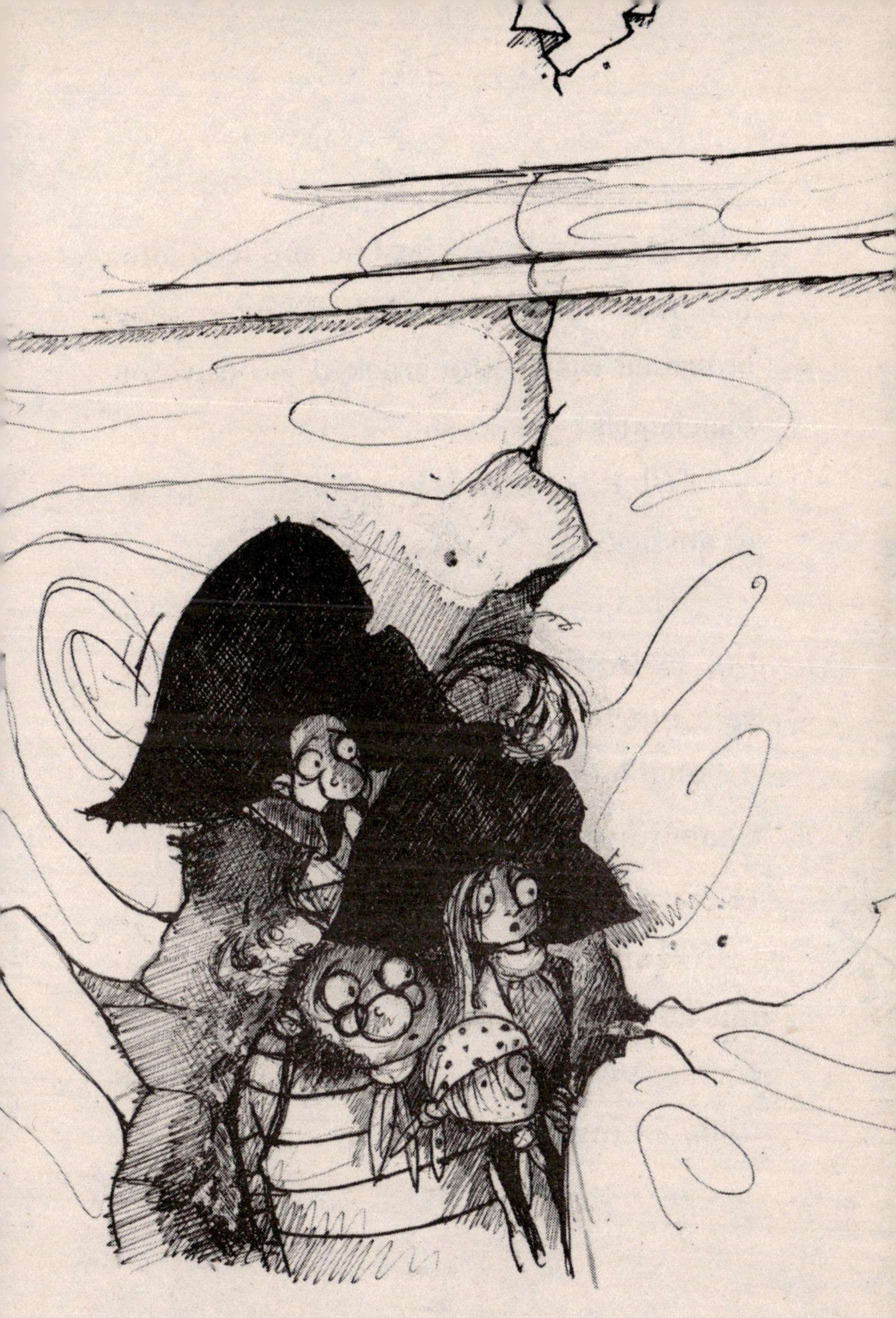

calling to Mr. Tooey to come and feed him.

“He’s hungry,” whispered Lily as they crouched inside the cracked wood of the baseboard.

“What splendid luck,” said Captain Crabsticks.

“This is our chance! We need to seize the moment while Doyle is distracted,” said Button.

Suddenly, everything went dark. Something was blocking the hole. Button reached out a hand. It felt like paper.

“Mr. Tooey . . .” Lily said.

They could hear the owner of the junk shop grumbling in the kitchen. He was complaining about how Doyle was always

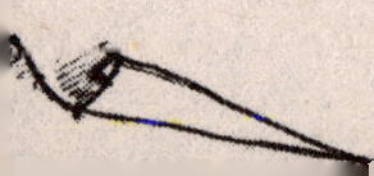

hungry and how food was always disappearing from the shelves in the middle of the night.

Button thought quickly. He tore a hole in the paper and climbed through.

"Where's Button gone?" said Uncle Noggin in surprise.

"It's all right! It's his grocery shopping!" came Button's muffled voice.

He was having a good look around inside Mr. Tooey's shopping bag. There was a tub of margarine, a stack of canned dog food, a box of tea bags, a pint of milk, and a loaf of bread.

"Huh, him and his horrible granary bread," came a voice from behind Button.

TEA
80

"Why does he keep buying that stuff? The bits get stuck in my teeth."

Lily had climbed through the hole and into the bag too.

"Quick, Lily, help me lift this margarine lid," Button said.

"What? We're not going in there . . . Are we?" Lily asked.

"Hurry," Button said. "We've only got seconds."

The two pirates grabbed the lip of the lid and pushed upward with all their might. It popped open and the smell of sunflower oil came wafting out. Button clambered through the gap between the lid and the tub, and plopped himself into the creamy mush. Lily pulled herself up and followed Button in.

"Ugh, it's all slimy," she complained as she pulled the lid back down on top of them.

"Get a move on," Button shouted to Uncle Noggin and Captain Crabsticks.

Too late.

The bag was lifted into the air. Button and Lily heard a metallic clank as a can of dog food was taken out and opened, and then they felt the margarine tub being taken out of the bag.

All at once, everything went very, very cold. Button felt a shiver go down his spine.

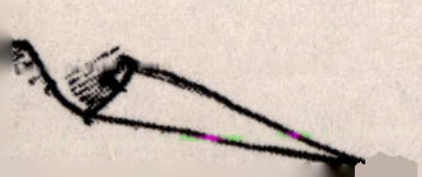

From the gap in the wall, the Captain was looking on in horror. Uncle Noggin had gone silent.

"Poor Lily and Button," said the Captain. "Lost and alone in Fridge. They'll be terrified without us. What now, my dear fellow?"

"We need a plan. . . ." Noggin replied thoughtfully.

"And I think I've got one!" the Captain exclaimed, slapping his thigh.

He pointed up at the table to where the open can of dog food was sitting.

"No . . . Really?" Noggin said.

"It's our only chance."

"I was hoping for something more . . . tasty!"

"Me too." The Captain shrugged. "But to be perfectly honest, I haven't tried dog food. You never know!"

And so they clambered through the gap in the wall and began to climb the notches and grains in the chair leg as fast as they could. Uncle Noggin puffed and panted and tried not to look down.

They had to be quick.

The Wooden Horse

Inside Fridge, Button was lying in the curl of a celery stick. He had used the celery leaves to wipe off the margarine and now he was chomping on a slice of honey roast ham. Celery was good for a lot of things, he thought, but it didn't taste as nice as ham.

They had found the cheese. A big old chunk of holey deliciousness. The food that pirates loved the best.

Button knew they would need a decent plan to get the cheese out of Fridge. Just for now, though, he and Lily were too tempted

by the choice of food available. Button had lost his breakfast to the woodlouse army, and knew that if he wasn't quick, he'd lose all the tastiest morsels in Fridge once

Uncle Noggin arrived. The only thing they couldn't eat was the cheese, as it had to be as big as possible when they handed it over to the mice.

Meanwhile, Uncle Noggin and the Captain had reached the tabletop, huffing and panting with the effort. Uncle Noggin slid a pepper pot up to the side of the can so that he could climb up and inside. The Captain had a quick look around for Mr. Tooey, and then quickly followed.

“I say, what’s that dreadful smell?” he said, after a squelchy landing.

“It tastes even worse,” said Uncle Noggin.

“My dear chap, you didn’t . . . Did you?’

“I did,” Uncle Noggin replied, looking a bit green.

Then the can tilted over to one side and lifted into the air.

"Take cover!" Captain Crabsticks ordered, and burrowed deeper into the dog food.

Button stared at the can that had just appeared on the shelf in Fridge, then jumped as the Captain's face peered over the side, followed by Uncle Noggin's.

"I think this is supposed to be chicken flavor," he said. "But I wouldn't recommend it."

They climbed out, smelling badly of the stinky pet food.

"It's given me gas," said Uncle Noggin.

“Everything gives you gas,” said Button, handing them both a celery leaf to wipe themselves down.

“I had to try it,” Uncle Noggin insisted. “I needed something inside me. I would have wasted away to nothing otherwise.” And then, distracted, he exclaimed, “Oooh, is that the cheese? It’s a beauty!”

As Button followed Uncle Noggin’s gaze, an idea suddenly hit him.

“What was that story you told me once?”

he asked. "Something about a big wooden horse. And soldiers . . . From that big book. You know—the one you got crushed inside a couple of weeks ago."

"Ah, you mean the one about the Trojan Horse?" Uncle Noggin grinned. "One of my favorites, that . . ."

He perched on a nearby mushroom, took a chunk from one side and between munches, began the story.

"Many many many years ago, the ancient Greeks were at war with people called the Trojans. One day, a huge horse made of wood was left at the gates of the Trojan city, Troy. The Trojans thought it was a peace offering from the Greek army, so they wheeled it inside the gates and admired it all day long. But what they didn't know was that the Greek army was hiding inside the horse's tummy. When darkness fell, the soldiers all climbed out of the horse. With their deadly weapons they took over the city and that was the end of Troy."

“Why do you want a story now, young fellow?” quizzed the Captain. “Aren’t we supposed to be thinking of a way to get inside the mice’s den?”

"I think Button has a plan, Cap'n sir . . . ," said Lily, grinning.

"Captain Crabsticks, please could you cut a hole in that cheese?" asked Button, still staring at the enormous lump.

"Of course. Niftiest sword on the Seven Seas, at your service," said the Captain, with a little bow.

"I mean a hole right out of the middle. You know, so it's hollow," Button continued.

"Ahhhhh . . . You mean like the wooden horse in the story?" said Uncle Noggin, tapping his nose.

"Exactly!" Button said.

"Button, you are a genius!" Lily exclaimed, clapping her hands, then realizing how cold they felt. "By the way, it's freezing in here. We need to get a move on."

And before they knew it, the Captain had drawn his sword and was carving his way into the middle of the hunk of cheese.

Everyone filled their mouths and their bags with tasty pieces. To the Pocket Pirates, good cheese was pure treasure. It was better than any gold or sparkling jewels.

When the lump was hollow, Button stood back and pondered. How would they lower the cheese to the floor? Then he had his second brilliant idea of the day.

Button pulled a shoelace from his bag and unrolled it. He threw one end over the rails of the shelf above, catching it as it came back down, then looped it around the cheese and tied it tightly. Lily and Uncle Noggin grabbed the other end of the shoelace and tugged hard.

"Heave-ho, crew!" cheered the Captain as the cheese rose into the air.

Button climbed on to the margarine tub and jumped aboard.

"Pull to the edge, please," he asked Uncle Noggin and Lily.

As the crew shuffled to the edge of the shelf, Button pulled on the shoelace to make the cheese swing. Then Lily and Uncle Noggin slowly let out the rope from their hands, lowering their cargo to the bottom shelf.

"Treasure ahoy!" shouted Lily.

Button slid down from the cheese, untied the shoelace, and stuffed it back into his bag.

"Now," he said cheerfully, "we just need to work out how to open the door and get out of here!"

Cheese on Wheels

Button held the huge stick of celery at one end, and at the other, the Captain and Lily wedged it into the seal of the door. Button pulled it back with Uncle Noggin's help and then, very slowly, the seal unstuck itself and the door gently opened.

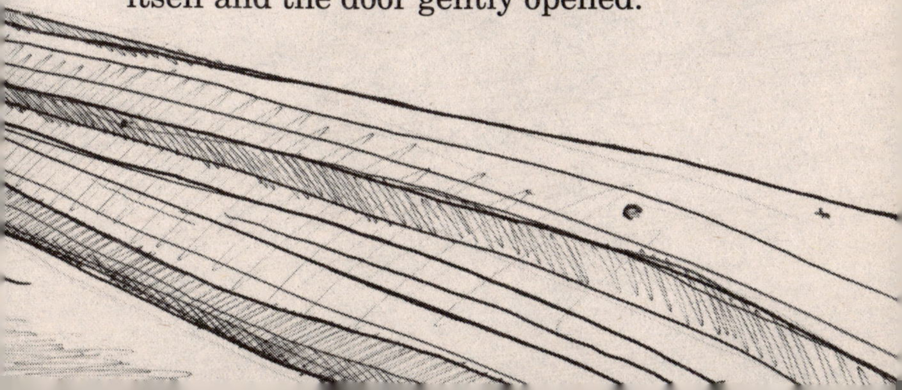

“Last chance for food shopping,” said Uncle Noggin, and as he shoved his face into a large pile of fancy chocolates, Button grabbed a slab of fresh fish from a packet

with clear plastic wrapped around it and stuffed it into his bag.

They carefully squeezed through the open door, pushing the cheese out of Fridge and on to the tiled floor.

"Uncle Noggin, I need you to head to the old toy box and wheel back the wooden train," Button instructed.

"I'll do my best, but I think I've eaten too much," Noggin admitted as he hobbled off.

"The other way . . ." said Lily, hiding a chuckle.

"Aye aye," he said. "So it is." And he set off in the opposite direction, puffing and blowing and trumping out loud.

The light was fading now. It was the perfect time of day to wheel the cheese down the hallway to the mice. Mr. Tooey wouldn't be back. A day in the shop always wore him out and they knew he would be resting in front of the TV in his favorite chair, trying not to nod off.

After what seemed like hours, Uncle Noggin returned, pushing the wooden toy train across the floor toward them.

"Are . . . you . . . ready . . . ?" asked Uncle Noggin who, by now, was panting even harder.

"We're ready," said Button and Lily.

Together, they heaved the large chunk of cheese onto the carriage. It was a bit too wide and wobbled unevenly in its place.

"It will be okay," said Uncle Noggin. "I'll take it slow."

Button grinned. All Uncle Noggin *ever* did was "take it slow."

"Shall we?" said Button, turning to Lily.

"Let's do it!" she replied. They threw their bags into the back of the train and climbed into the hole that Captain Crabsticks had expertly carved into the cheese. Then Uncle Noggin picked up the slice that made the door to cover them up and he fastened it into place.

“Are you okay in there?” he said.

“Shipshape,” said Lily.

Button couldn’t answer. His mouth was already full of cheese.

“Ladies and gentlemen, the train now leaving the kitchen is the six forty-five service to Mouse Hole,” Noggin announced. “Please join for connections to Book Shelf and Toy Box.”

“Well done, old thing,” said the Captain. “You’d be a splendid train driver, if you weren’t a pirate!’

Uncle Noggin gave a little “TOOT TOOT” and began to push from the back. Captain Crabsticks steered from the front and off they went.

All seemed to be going smoothly until, as they rounded the corner into a puddle of light cast by a streetlamp outside the shop window, the Captain suddenly stopped.

“Oh crumbs,” he winced.

“What’s wrong, shipmate?” asked Uncle Noggin from the back, still trying to push the train.

"D-D-Doyle. Abandon ship!"

The dark shape of a dog loomed in front of them. It sniffed and came closer.

"Crew, it's been an honor to be your captain," said Captain Crabsticks bravely, straightening up, ready to face his doom.

"Eh?" said Button from inside the cheese.

Doyle's face was now level with the Captain's. A long pink tongue shot out of the dog's slobbering mouth. . . .

"Cap'n! I'm coming!" shouted Noggin, hobbling toward them as fast as he could.

But before Noggin could do anything, the dog started licking the Captain from head to toe, covering him in drool. After a

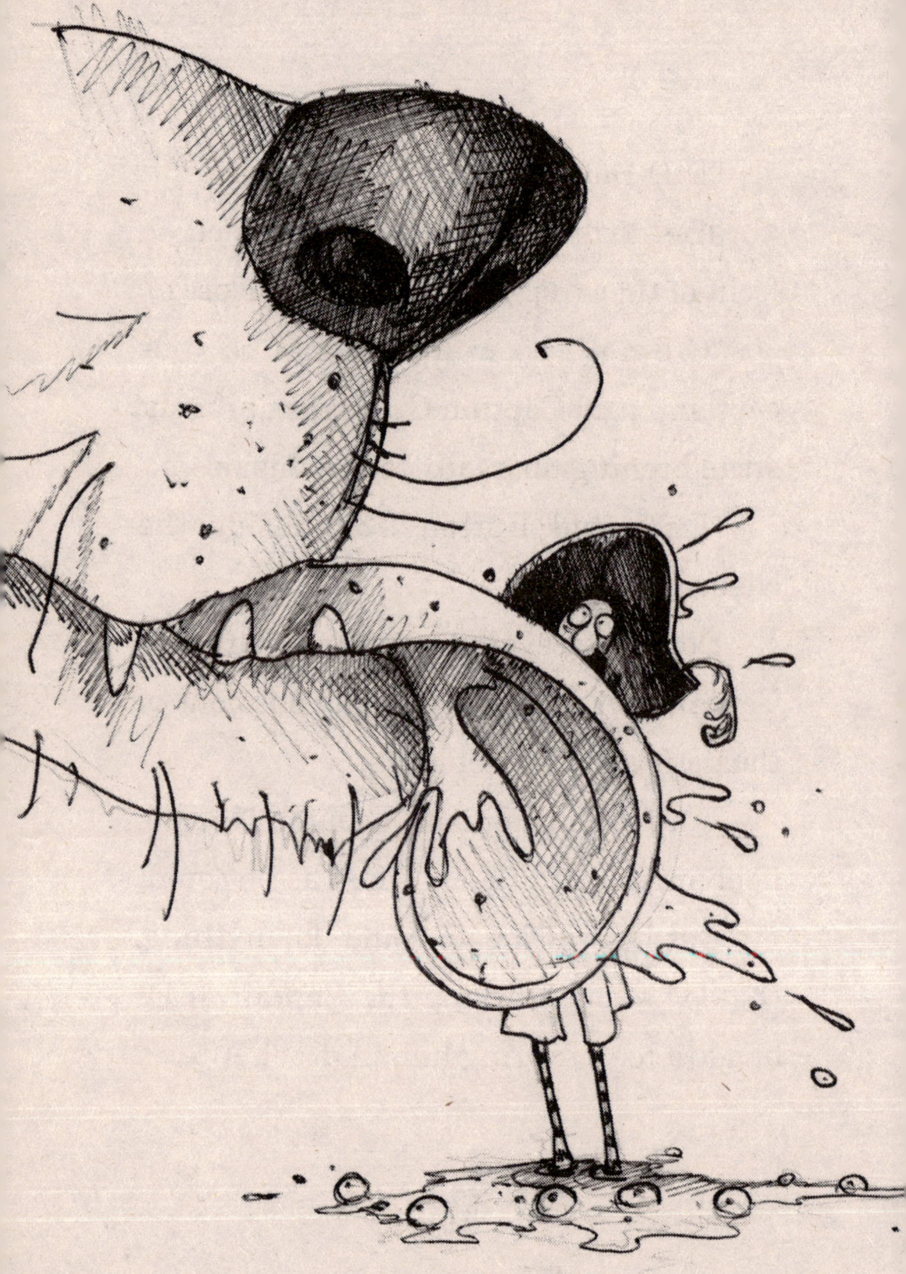

few long licks, Doyle wandered back into the dark kitchen.

"Er . . . Captain, are you still alive?" asked Button.

"I think so . . ." the Captain said. "Must have been the dog food he could smell."

"Phew," gasped Uncle Noggin. "Thought you were a goner, sir."

"This ship won't go down without a fight!" the Captain cheered. "And now for those dreadful mice!"

Cat Burgling

"The wooden horse has arrived at the gates of Troy," whispered Uncle Noggin. It was his way of telling Button and Lily that they had arrived.

Lily and Button were ready to leap out of the cheese if Jones was handed over and ready to stay put if he wasn't.

Captain Crabsticks stood at the entrance to the mouse hole. Then he took his sword and tapped it against the broken wooden doorway.

Something poked him in the back. The Captain turned around to find himself nose to snout with Pepper Jack. The mouse had been hiding outside the hole, waiting for them to turn up.

Everyone knew that Captain Crabsticks was an old softy, but he was also fearless. He raised his sword slowly, pointing it toward Pepper Jack's pink button nose.

"Now, listen here, you old scratcher. We've brought you your cheese. So let's be having our ship's cat back. Do you hear me?"

Pepper Jack made no sound. He simply pushed the Captain's blade aside with a single claw. Then he lifted the Captain and

pinned him against the baseboard. The Captain couldn't move.

Uncle Noggin mustered up all his bravery and thundered toward the mouse, only to be whipped off his feet by Pepper Jack's huge tail.

The other mice poured out of the mouse hole, sniffing and searching. Their tails winding and curling and their long noses

poking here and there. They took hold of the cheese and dragged it inside their den, but there was no sign of Jones.

Just then, Doyle came padding across the shop floor toward them. In a flash,

Pepper Jack released his grip on the Captain and shot inside the hole. Crabsticks was left in a heap on the floor, watching helplessly as Doyle gave Uncle Noggin a thorough licking. The old pirate had been covered in pet food too. Then the dog wandered off again and curled up in his basket.

"At least we're on good terms with Doyle," said Uncle Noggin. "But now we need to get in there and find Button and Lily."

"Don't worry about them," said the Captain. "They can handle this. *I've* got a plan. . . . Now, where is that book on pest control? I was reading it only earlier. . . ."

"WHAT? We're in the middle of a crisis and you want to read?" said Uncle Noggin.

"Trust me, old chap," Captain Crabsticks said, looking at the bookshelves high above them. "Ah, there it is. Help me get up to that shelf, would you?"

In the mice's den, Lily and Button sat huddled inside the cheese, filled with fear. The mice had rolled the cheese through the mouse hole and when they came to a stop, the doorway Captain Crabsticks had carved was facing the floor. There was no way to escape.

The little pirates listened as the mice clawed and nibbled at the cheese from the outside, waiting for them to burst through.

Button's tummy gave a sudden rumble.

"I can't believe you are thinking about food at a time like this," whispered Lily in surprise.

"Hang on, it's given me an idea. . . ." said Button. "Hope you're hungry too!"

And he turned around and started to dig his way out at the back. He pulled chunks of cheese out of the wall with his hands and stuffed them straight into his mouth.

"It needs both of us," he said, his

cheeks full, and so Lily began to dig in too. She clawed lumps with her hands and ate as much as she could.

Soon there was a hole big enough for Button to wriggle out. As Button grabbed Lily by her hands and pulled her through, claws pierced the wall of the cheese behind them.

It was pitch black. They could see nothing. It smelled foul and they could feel large soft shapes around their feet.

Mouse poo. The smell was so strong they felt sick. They only had minutes before the mice realized they were there. Where was Jones?

They felt their way around, the sound of their movement drowned out by the chattering of mice teeth. Button kept one hand clutched around Lily's coattail, desperate not to lose her. Ahead of him, she kept feeling her way until a passageway showed itself. They followed it, not knowing where it might lead.

It was only by chance that they bumped into an old box. Something moved inside it. It was worth a try. "Help me," Button whispered to Lily. "It's heavy."

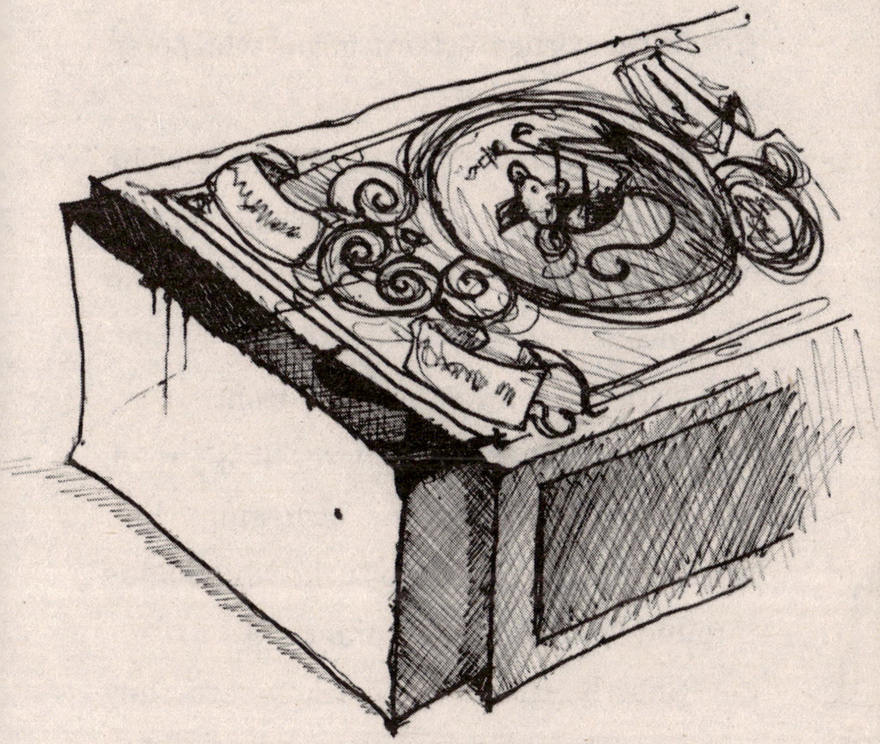

Together they pulled the inside drawer out of the box. Button felt inside and to his surprise there was something furry curled up in the corner. A faint meow whispered in the darkness.

Button smiled. “Come on, old boy,” he said, pulling Jones out of the box and giving him a cuddle. He felt a warm lick on his face.

“Ergh, you stink,” said Button.

“Time to get out of here,” Lily urged, and grabbed Button, dragging him through the dark as he tucked his hands around Jones and held him tight.

Shortly, they were back where they started. The cheese was now in little piles all over the floor, but it meant the pirates could see the entrance to the mouse hole.

The sniffing got louder, as if the mice had sensed something strange in their home.

"Run!" yelled Lily and they burst into full speed, racing toward the hole in the baseboard. The menacing mice were on their tail, scampering as fast as they could after the Pocket Pirates. Button was so full of cheese he could feel it churning around inside him as he ran.

"Faster!" cried Lily, from the front. Button could feel the mice's stinky breath down the back of his neck.

Meanwhile, up on the bookshelf, Captain Crabsticks could just about hear the commotion below.

"Brace yourself, old bean!" he told Uncle Noggin.

They watched as Lily and Button burst out through the baseboard hole, racing across the hallway floor.

"NOW!" the Captain yelled, and between them, he and Uncle Noggin sent the copy of *Domestic Pest Control* hurtling down to the ground, just as the mice shot out of their hole. The heavy book landed on top of the mice with a *crash*.

Lily and Button whirled round at the *thud* behind them and couldn't believe

their eyes. They looked up and cheered as they spotted Captain Crabsticks and Uncle Noggin on the bookshelf, hopping around and waving their arms in glee.

Dazed squeaks and squeals were coming from beneath the book, but the two Pocket Pirates didn't stop to find out what the mice would do next. They scooted off in the direction of the fireplace, waving at their shipmates to follow.

A Good Wash

Button had to scale the shelves and boxes to get to the top and wind the musical box lift. No one could do it as quickly as he could. Not even Lily, and she was fast.

Jones was hanging on tightly to Button. The little cat purred into Button's

chest as he climbed over all the odds and ends like a scurrying insect.

There was nothing that beat a wild adventure, but returning home to a warm candle stub and an upturned thumbtack of cake crumbs came pretty close. The cozy safety of his hammock onboard the ship still seemed a world away, but Button knew he would soon be there, lying back and dreaming of life on the ocean waves. Dry land was more dangerous than being at sea, it seemed.

"It's all right, Jones, you can let go now!" Button said to the cat. "You poor old thing, you look like you need a good meal and a good wash."

He took the slice of fish from his bag and fed it to Jones. The little cat gobbled it down and carried on licking Button's hands. "Sorry," Button told him, "I don't have any more fish. But I'll tell you what I do have. . . ."

He headed into the corner of the shelf, returning with one of the pots of coffee cream he had kept by for a special occasion. He opened it carefully, peeling back the foil top. Then he dipped a nutshell inside and handed the cat a generous helping.

Below, the others waited eagerly. They'd had enough of hanging around below the shelf. Lily was in position, hold-

ing on to the cotton. She had impatiently tugged on it several times already.

"All right, all right! I'm here," insisted Button.

He wound the handle of the musical box. It took some strength and it had to be wound up fully for the passenger to reach the top. Soon Button saw Lily's grinning face appearing.

"Thanks, Button," she said as she jumped back onto the shelf.

The musical box played a tinkly tune as the cotton wound itself back down to the remaining crewmates. Then, when Uncle Noggin had tugged on the thread, Button began turning again.

Button strained to turn the handle, feeling all the cheese churning in his tummy again. Lily joined him and they heaved and heaved, pulling as hard as they could.

"Maybe Uncle Noggin's eaten too much cheese as well!" Lily suggested.

Eventually, Uncle Noggin appeared and the three of them hauled the Captain up together.

"Aye aye, Captain. All present and accounted for, sir," said Button.

"Well done, young Button," said the Captain. "But what is that HORRIBLE smell?"

"It's us!" said Button. "We smell of fish, and pet food and dog drool. . . ."

"And cheese!" added Lily.

"In that case, it's baths all round, I'm afraid," said Captain Crabsticks. "I know we've all had one this year already, but this is a special occasion. Button, you know your duties. Off you go."

And so Button headed off to the old mustard jar at the back of the shelf. He pried off the lid with a broken matchstick and pulled the tiny piece of cork out of the leaky pipe until hot water had filled their bathtub.

He took the lens cleaning cloth from the case with the broken glasses and scraped a slice of soap from the quarter of a bar that they kept behind the bottle.

While the others sat down and lit the candle, he jumped in and scrubbed himself clean. Then he let the water out into

the plant pot and filled another bathtub for Lily, while the Captain and Old Uncle Noggin had a sneaky nap.

Button sat down next to Jones and tickled him under his chin. The ship's cat gave a rumbly purr and promptly fell into a contented sleep. His adventure was over!

Back on the Shelf

Mr. Tooey was scratching his head. There had been too many unexplained goings-on just recently. Somehow, *Domestic Pest Control* had fallen off the shelf all on its own, and now, a wooden train from the toy box had found its way into the middle of the hallway. The train was full of crumbs

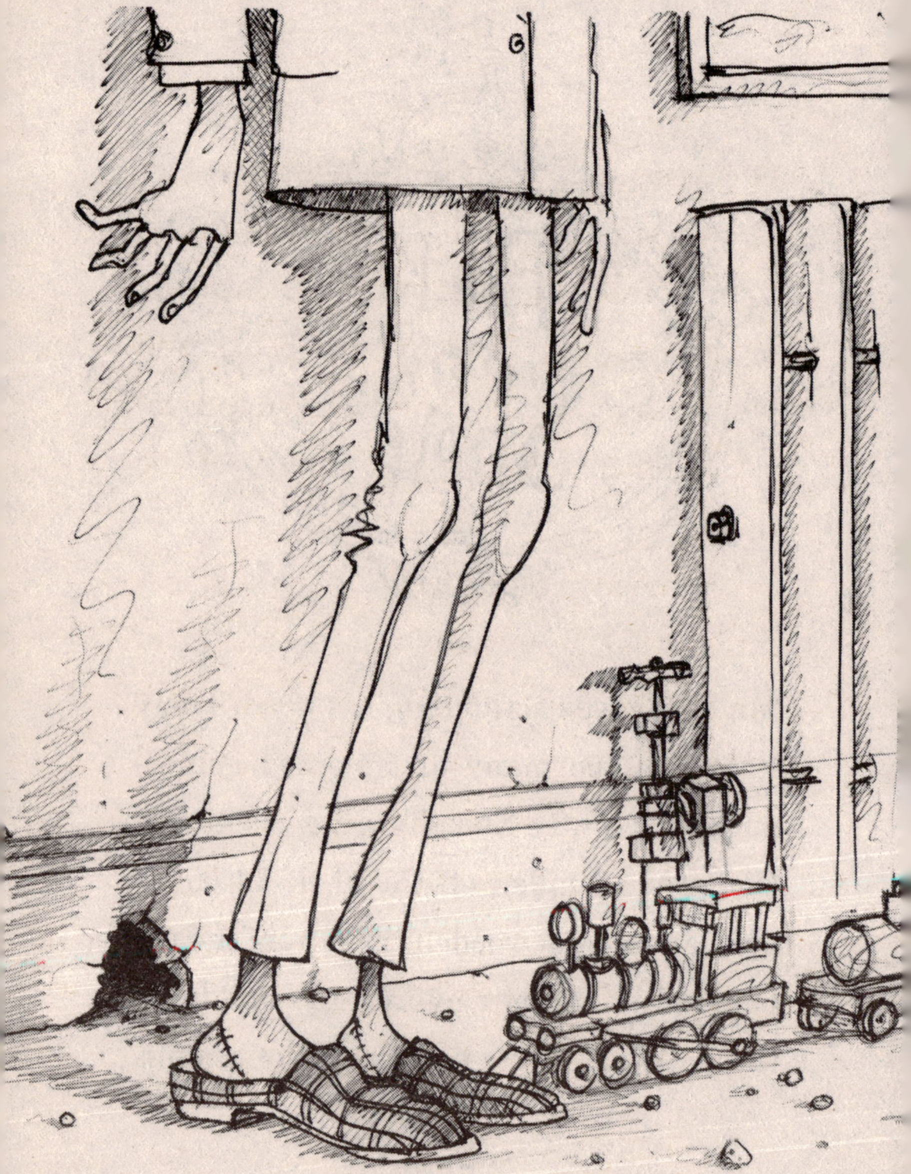

of cheese and, when he thought about it, he was sure he had heard strange noises coming from the baseboard. . . . Did he have mice that liked to read books and play with toy trains? he wondered to himself, then chuckled at the silliness of the thought.

He headed to the fridge to make something to eat. But when he got to the tub of margarine, right there in the middle were the imprints of two tiny people. Arms and legs and heads.

Mr. Tooey blinked hard in disbelief and headed to the room at the back for a lie down. Maybe he was going crazy after all. . . .

In the mouse hole in the baseboard, Pepper Jack sat staring up at the Pocket Pirates' shelf. The mice had won themselves some tasty cheese, but nonetheless, Pepper Jack was mad that the little pirates had foiled him. He watched as Button raised the pirate flag high. They would never foil him again, Pepper Jack thought with a scowl, and he turned and sloped back into the mice's den.

The Pocket Pirates were sitting around the candle stub. Uncle Noggin rubbed his stomach and gave a great big sigh.

"Ahhhh. It's nice to be back," he said as

he lay back on a bed of cotton wool. "What a long day."

Jones had a stomach full of fish and was curled up snug and warm under the glow of the candlelight. Button stroked his head and listened to him purr.

"Let's look at the booty then," said the Captain, and they all emptied their bags and pockets out onto the shelf. "Well, well, we've done ourselves proud. That's a fine hoard of treasure if ever I saw one."

There was enough cheese to last three weeks, a sackful of fresh biscuit crumbs, a sizeable chunk of milk chocolate that had given Captain Crabsticks a bad back,

and three pocketfuls of chicken bits.

And it didn't stop there. They had a large green olive, a spectacularly meaty corner of pizza and three whole peanuts. It was a feast!

"Tally-ho! Get in there," said the Captain. "What's the matter with you all?"

"We're stuffed," groaned Button. "I've eaten far too much cheese, not to mention all the ham."

"Ham?" said Uncle Noggin, sitting upright in surprise. "I didn't see any ham!"

"That's because Button ate it before you got to Fridge," Lily said with a chuckle.

And so the Pocket Pirates, stuffed and smelling lovely after their baths, headed back into their ship in a bottle and settled down to sleep. Just before

Button closed his eyes, he looked over at Lily and she gave him a grin.

Who knew what new adventures would await them in the morning?

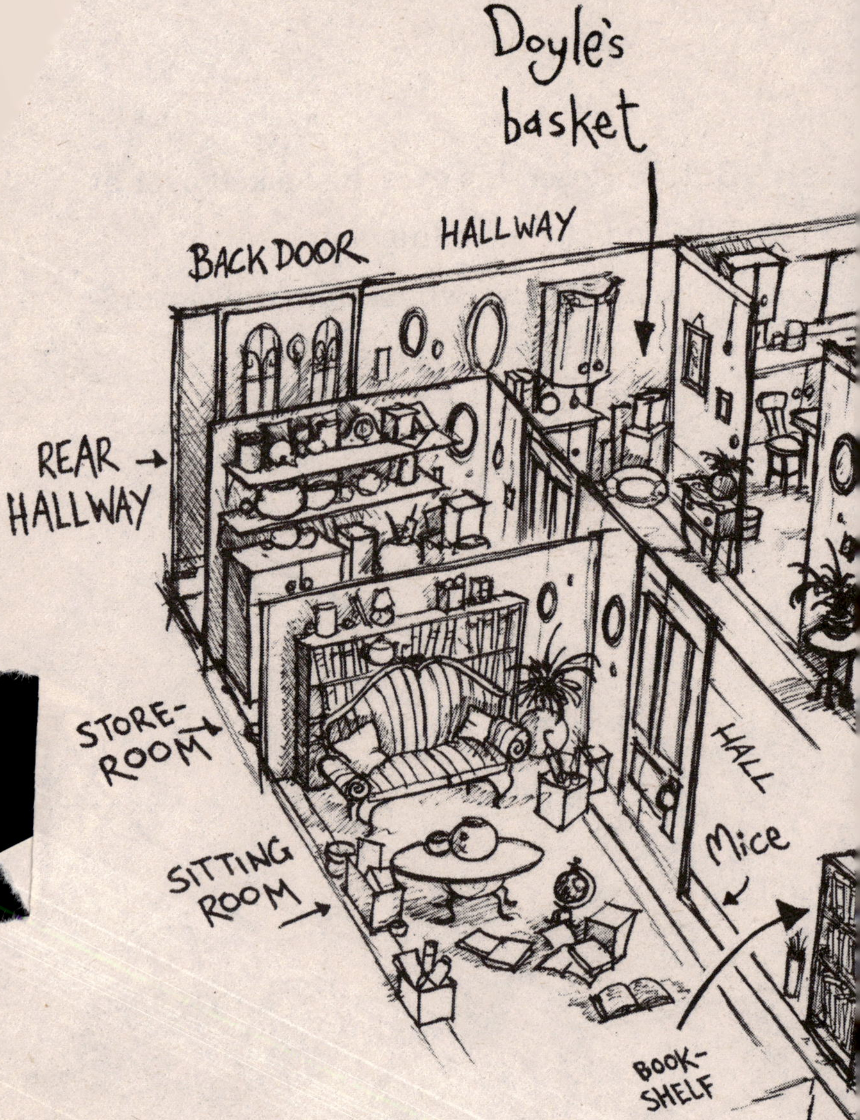
Doyle's basket
BACK DOOR
HALLWAY
REAR HALLWAY
STORE-ROOM
SITTING ROOM
HALL
Mice
BOOK-SHELF

The place called Fridge (Here be treasure).
The broken plug
KITCHEN
SHOP
The Ship in the Bottle
SHOP
12
SHOP WINDOW
FRONT DOOR
N
W
E
S
The Old JUNKSHOP

Turn the page for a peek at Book 2
in the Pocket Pirates adventures:

THE GREAT DRAIN ESCAPE

Things were not going too well for Button the ship's boy. He was trapped in sticky webbing, unable to move, and six hungry eyes, eight spindly legs, and a mouth full of spiky fangs were heading in his direction. Mr. Dregby, the house spider, had finally caught the young Pocket Pirate in his trap, and it was time for dinner.

Mr. Dregby slowly lowered himself toward Button, dangling from his spider silk. He stretched out four of his eight legs, reaching for the little pirate.

Button wriggled as hard as he could, desperately trying to free himself, and then—

THUMP!

He fell out of his hammock and woke up.

"Sufferin' lobster lumps," he gasped, rubbing his eyes and getting to his feet. "That was a *horrible* dream."

Button decided it would be a sensible idea to climb out of the ship in a bottle and take a good look around the shelf. He

needed to be sure Mr. Dregby was safely tucked away in his corner, and not on the lookout for a Pocket Pirate–size snack.

As he slipped out through the neck of the bottle and down to the wooden shelf, he was met with a lovely surprise. The sun was shining in through the window of the old junk shop. It was a beautiful day, and perfect for exploring.

There was a loud rumbling sound.

Button looked down. “Oh dear, it’s my stomach again,” he groaned.

Supplies were low at the moment. The poor pirate crew had barely eaten for days. They were getting by on stale breadcrumbs and a piece of moldy old cheese left over from their last adventure. And that wasn’t really enough to fill the tummies of four pirates and one ship's cat. Old Uncle Noggin and Captain Crabsticks were big eaters, and the youngest member of the crew, Lily, could pack away the grub too. Button had even tried chewing on the leaves of a potted plant, but that had left him with a terrible tummy ache.

The problem had started when the owner of the junk shop, Mr. Tooey, had moved Doyle's basket under the Pocket Pirates' shelf. The shipmates needed to find a different way down to floor level that avoided the sly, slobbery dog.

The only thing Doyle was good for was keeping the evil baseboard mice at bay. Who knows what might happen if

the mice got hold of the pirates? And they often tried! But the Pocket Pirates *had* to leave the shelf soon, or they would starve.

Button was still pondering when Lily appeared. She gave him a stern look. She could always tell when he was plotting something.

"I'd like some fresh air," Button announced.

"Pardon?" Lily said. "I don't think that's a good idea. . . . Remember what happened last time you went off on your own? Your coat got caught on that picture hook and you were nearly Mr. Dregby's dinner!"

Button wasn't put off. "Maybe you should come with me?" he suggested. "We

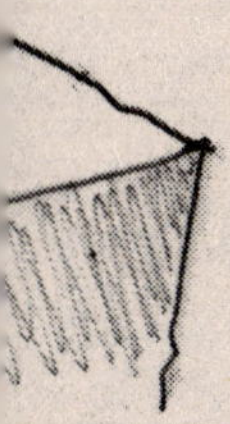

could go hunting outside for breakfast and be back before the Captain and Old Uncle Noggin are awake."

Lily folded her arms and gave Button an even sterner look. "Out into the street? Are you nuts? We can't even get down from the shelf now that Doyle has moved!"

"But there must be another way down, and we're sooooo *hungry*," Button said, rubbing his tummy. "You never know what we might find out there. Once, when Uncle Noggin was younger, he found a lump of fish and three fries inside an old newspaper."

Lily made a *hmph* sound and rolled her eyes.

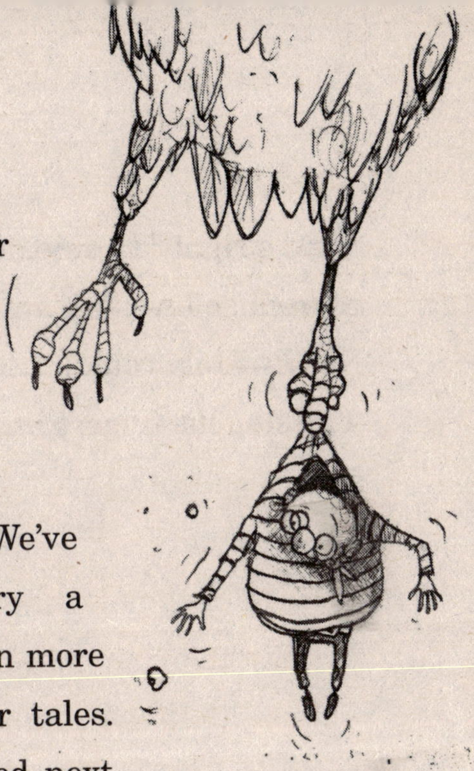

"Did you hear me, Lily?" Button said. "FISH . . . AND . . . FRIES!"

"Yes, I heard you!" said Lily. "We've heard that story a million times. Even more than all his other tales. But what happened next, Button? He was attacked by a pigeon! Carried away and left up a tree. He's still got the scars to prove it. You know I like adventure as much as the next pirate, but it's too dangerous out there!"

Button gave Lily a solemn look. "Okay,

you're right," he said. "It *is* too dangerous. I promise I won't leave the shelf."

But Lily couldn't see that Button was crossing his fingers behind his back.